Time to Play
Janine Scott
AF583985

It is time to play.
The baby bears
climb up a tree.

It is time to play.
The baby foxes
hide in the grass.

It is time to play.
The baby elephants
splash in the water.

It is time to play.
The baby polar bears
roll in the snow.

It is time to play.
The baby lions
jump over a log.

It is time to sleep.
The baby lions sleep on a rock.